Nonfiction

OKLAHOMA CITY THUNDER

by Ray Frager

Published by ABDO Publishing Company, 8000 West 78th Street, Edina, Minnesota 55439. Copyright © 2012 by Abdo Consulting Group, Inc. International copyrights reserved in all countries. No part of this book may be reproduced in any form without written permission from the publisher. SportsZone™ is a trademark and logo of ABDO Publishing Company.

Printed in the United States of America,
North Mankato, Minnesota
062011
092011

 THIS BOOK CONTAINS AT LEAST 10% RECYCLED MATERIALS.

Editor: Seth Putnam
Copy Editor: Anna Comstock
Series design: Christa Schneider
Cover production: Craig Hinton
Interior production: Carol Castro

Photo Credits: Alonzo Adams/AP Images, cover; Thearon Henderson/AP Images, 1; Eric Gay/AP Images, 4; Ted S. Warren/AP Images, 7, 43 (middle); Sue Ogrocki/AP Images, 8, 47; AP Images, 10, 13, 16, 19, 20, 22, 25, 27, 42 (top, bottom); Ron Wurzer/AP Images, 14, 42 (middle); Dave Tenenbaum/AP Images, 28; Grant M. Haller/AP Images, 31; Gary Stewart/AP Images, 32, 43 (top); Elaine Thompson/AP Images, 35; Pat Sullivan/AP Images, 36; Kevork Djansezian/AP Images, 38; Alex Gallardo/AP Images, 41, 43 (bottom); Michael Conroy/AP Images, 44

Library of Congress Cataloging-in-Publication Data
Frager, Ray.
 Oklahoma City Thunder / by Ray Frager.
   p. cm. -- (Inside the NBA)
 Includes index.
 ISBN 978-1-61783-169-0
 1. Oklahoma City Thunder (Basketball team)--History--Juvenile literature. I. Title.
 GV885.52.O37F73 2012
 796.323'640976638--dc23
                              2011021688

TABLE OF CONTENTS

Chapter 1 .... A Thundering Shake-up, 4

Chapter 2 .... Humble Beginnings, 10

Chapter 3 .... Hints of Greatness, 16

Chapter 4 .... Champions at Last, 22

Chapter 5 .... Regular Contenders, 28

Chapter 6 .... New City, New Future, 36

Timeline, 42

Quick Stats, 44

Quotes and Anecdotes, 45

Glossary, 46

For More Information, 47

Index, 48

About the Author, 48

CHAPTER 1

A THUNDERING SHAKE-UP

If it had not been for Hurricane Katrina, there might not be a professional basketball team in Oklahoma City, Oklahoma.

After the hurricane devastated New Orleans, Louisiana, the city's National Basketball Association (NBA) team, the Hornets, needed a new place to play temporarily. That place was Oklahoma City.

The Hornets played most of their home games in the 2005–06 and 2006–07 seasons in Oklahoma City. In fact, for those two years the team was officially known as the New Orleans/Oklahoma City Hornets. Oklahoma City responded enthusiastically to the Hornets. The team quickly ranked in the NBA's top third in attendance. Though there was some discussion about the Hornets permanently moving to Oklahoma City, the team eventually returned to New Orleans.

The Oklahoma City Thunder's Russell Westbrook dunks against the Dallas Mavericks on May 23, 2011.

SHOOTING STAR

Kevin Durant quickly showed himself to be one of the NBA's best players. In addition to his performance for the Thunder, Durant was a member of the US team in the International Basketball Federation (FIBA) World Championships in 2010. He led the US team to the championship.

Despite his talent, Durant has publicly refrained from boasting about himself. When his Team USA teammate Dwight Howard said he would take Durant over superstar LeBron James, Durant replied: "As a competitor, as a guy who's real with myself, I don't think I'm on LeBron's level yet. I'm working, though." And his hard work is paying off. During the 2009–10 regular season, Durant recorded 2,472 points, 623 rebounds, and 231 assists. He scored 30.1 points per game and made 90 percent of his free throws.

Meanwhile, the owner of the Seattle SuperSonics, Howard Shultz, was not happy with the situation at his team's arena. The club was not making enough money. So Schultz sold the team to a group of businessmen from Oklahoma City in July 2006. That group, led by Clay Bennett, head of the Professional Basketball Club LLC group, said it planned to keep the Sonics in Seattle. But the owners would only keep the team there if they could get a new arena. That was a big "if."

After a year, there was no promise of a new arena in Seattle. Washington state lawmakers did not pass a plan to build one that year. The owners began to talk about moving the team. On November 2, 2007, they asked the NBA to let them take the Sonics to Oklahoma City. The league's

Howard Schultz, *left*, former owner of the SuperSonics, presents a jersey to Oklahoma City businessman Clay Bennett.

owners approved the move on April 18, 2008.

Seattle did not let the team just pack up and move, though. The city went to court to try to stop the Sonics from leaving. City officials said the team had to honor the two years it had left on its lease at KeyArena. In June 2008, the team owners and the city went before a judge to argue the case. However, the judge did not get to decide who was right. On July 2, the two sides made a deal out of court.

The deal allowed the Sonics to move to Oklahoma City. But as part of the settlement, the team had to leave behind its name and colors in case another team was ever formed in Seattle. The former Sonics'

Thunder center Johan Petro (27) goes up for a shot against the Minnesota Timberwolves in Oklahoma City on November 2, 2008.

team was only nameless for a short time. The squad debuted in the 2008–09 season as the Oklahoma City Thunder. Their colors were blue and orange, and their mascot was "Rumble the Bison."

The Thunder played their first official NBA game on October 29, 2008, at the Ford Center in Oklahoma City. Before the game, the team hosted a party outside the arena. NBA commissioner

New Identity

Oklahoma City Mayor Mick Cornett thought the Thunder had given the city a new image. Previously, he said most people identified the city with the 1995 bombing of a federal building that killed 168 people. "When you say the words 'Oklahoma City,' the next word out of your mouth is probably 'bombing.' Having a major sports team helps identify our city with something positive," he said.

> ### Missing the Sonics
>
> "It's depressing that there is no trip to Seattle this year and there is no team in that city. There is a great history, and they certainly had some great players there. And now, there is no team left. It's sad."
> —NBA player Brent Barry, a former member of the SuperSonics, on not having a team in Seattle

David Stern welcomed the city to the NBA in a pre-game speech. Then, a sellout crowd of 19,136 watched the Thunder lose to the Milwaukee Bucks.

The Thunder nearly sold out every home game during the 2008–09 season. However, they did not find as much success on the court. The Thunder had just a 23–59 record. Coach P. J. Carlesimo was fired after the team's 1–12 start. Scott Brooks replaced him.

There was some hope, though. The team showed off a core of young players who looked ready to emerge as NBA stars. The most promising was Kevin Durant. In his second professional season, Durant averaged 25.3 points per game. At a slim 6 feet 9 inches and 215 pounds, Durant had just turned 20 at the start of 2008–09. Listed as a forward, Durant often played more like a guard because he shot from long range and drove to the basket. His long arms helped him get shots off against just about any opponent.

Fellow second-year forward Jeff Green and rookie guard Russell Westbrook averaged 16.5 and 15.3 points per game respectively. Westbrook also averaged 5.3 assists per game. Despite the team's poor record during its first season in Oklahoma City, fans had enthusiasm for a young team on the rise. But the team had not yet returned to the glory it had enjoyed in Seattle.

CHAPTER 2
HUMBLE BEGINNINGS

In December 1966, the NBA announced that it was expanding to Seattle. The team, which would begin playing in 1967, would be the first major professional team to play in that city. The club held a contest to come up with a name for the new team.

Because Seattle was home to Boeing, a company that builds airplanes, the winning suggestion was SuperSonics. Boeing built a plane called the Supersonic Transport.

The SuperSonics got off to a rough start. With a mostly young roster, they went just 23–59 during their first season, in 1967–68. They did have two high-quality players, though. Fourth-year guard Walt Hazzard averaged 24 points and 6.2 assists per game during the Sonics' first season. He finished in the NBA's top 10 in scoring. Bob Rule, a rookie center, scored 18.1 points and grabbed 9.5 rebounds per game.

Lenny Wilkens (19) of the Seattle SuperSonics passes off as he finds Billy Cunningham of the 76ers too much to shoot over in a 1971 game.

HUMBLE BEGINNINGS

The Sonics had their problems stopping other teams from scoring. They gave up at least 150 points in each of five games during the season. In one of those games, the Philadelphia 76ers scored 160 points.

The Sonics traded Hazzard to the Atlanta Hawks before their second season. In return they received Lenny Wilkens, a savvy point guard who was entering his 10th season in the NBA. The Sonics showed some improvement and won 30 games 1968–69. Rule had an even bigger season. He averaged 24 points per game to rank sixth in the league. He also averaged 11.5 rebounds per game. Wilkens, the team's All-Star player that year, scored 22.4 points per game. His 8.2 assists per game were second best in the NBA. Still, the team was going through growing pains. The Sonics endured a stretch of losing 18 out of 20 games early in the season.

For the 1969–70 season, Wilkens continued to play, but the Sonics also named him as their coach. The team got a little better, going 36–46. Wilkens averaged 17.8 points and led the team with 9.1 assists per game. That was the most assists in the NBA that season. Rule continued his high-scoring ways, as well. He averaged 24.6 points

> ### What Could Have Been
>
> After Bob Rule suffered a serious leg injury early in the 1970–71 season with Seattle, he was no longer the star forward/center he had once been. Rule played a few more years in the NBA, but he was out of the league by 1974. After two seasons of averaging 24 and 24.6 points per game for Seattle, Rule averaged 15.1 points per game in 1971–72, most of which he played for the Philadelphia 76ers. He never played close to a full season again, and he did not come close to averaging in double figures.

The Sonics' Zaid Abdul-Aziz (35) dribbles the ball around the Boston Celtics' Dave Cowens as he moves in for a shot on February 6, 1972.

and pulled down 10.3 rebounds per game.

The next season, the SuperSonics showed only slight improvement. They won just two more games than they had the year before. Still, that was impressive considering leading scorer Rule suffered a season-ending leg injury in the fourth game. The scoring slack created by Rule's absence was picked up by new arrival Spencer Haywood. He averaged 20.6 points per game. Wilkens added 19.8 points per game, and Dick Snyder scored 19.4 points per game.

Haywood jumped onto the Sonics' roster after one season in the American Basketball Association (ABA). He could not play for Seattle right away, though. At the time, the NBA had a rule against letting anyone play in the league until his

Spencer Haywood, *right*, former Seattle SuperSonics player, hoists his jersey into the rafters at KeyArena in 2007.

college class would have graduated. This meant a player was not allowed into the NBA until four years after he graduated from high school. Haywood had joined the ABA's Denver Rockets after his sophomore year of college, so he still had one more year before he would be NBA eligible. The Sonics went to court to challenge the NBA rule and won. Haywood then joined the team in time to play 33 games in 1970–71.

In 1971–72, the Sonics had Haywood for the full season. It was the team's best yet. They went 47–35, though they did not make the playoffs. Haywood ranked fourth in the NBA with 26.2 points per game. He also added 12.7 rebounds per game.

However, the Sonics did not build on that success during the next season. The team's owner, Sam Schulman, told Wilkens he could no longer be both a player and the coach. Wilkens had to choose. He picked player. Schulman decided Wilkens probably would not be able to handle playing for a new coach. So the Sonics traded Wilkens to the Cleveland Cavaliers.

"I thought I would give my full support to the coach," Wilkens said, "and I figured anyone who knew me would know that."

Without Wilkens as either player or coach, the Sonics sunk to just 26–56 in 1972–73. Haywood had an outstanding season, though. His 29.2-point scoring average ranked third in the NBA. His average of 12.9 rebounds per game was 10th. Haywood set a team record with 51 points against the Kansas City-Omaha Kings during one game in the season. Things were starting to heat up.

THE "HARDSHIP" RULE

Spencer Haywood left college after two years to join the ABA. He joined the NBA and the SuperSonics one year later. Haywood and the Sonics challenged the NBA's rule against permitting players into the league before completing four years of college.

Haywood claimed "hardship." He needed to earn money because of his family's poor financial situation. After the NBA lost to Haywood and the SuperSonics in court, it set up the hardship rule in 1971. Players could enter the league if they showed a financial need. The league did away with the hardship rule in 1976. After that, some players such as LeBron James and Kobe Bryant skipped college altogether and went straight to the pros. But in 2006, the NBA decided players could only declare for the draft if they were at least 19 years old and one year out of high school.

CHAPTER 3

HINTS OF GREATNESS

The SuperSonics struggled through the 1972–73 season under coaches Tom Nissalke and Bucky Buckwalter. So they brought in Bill Russell as the coach and general manager in 1973–74. As a player, Russell had led the Boston Celtics to 11 championships in 13 seasons.

The team immediately improved under Russell. The Sonics won 10 more games than they had the previous season for a 36–46 record. Spencer Haywood played like an All-Star, posting averages of 23.5 points and 13.4 rebounds per game. Both averages were in the NBA's top 10. In his third season, Freddie Brown established himself as one of the league's best long-range shooters. He averaged 16.5 points per game. His ability to score from way outside earned Brown the nickname "Downtown," as if his shots came from that far away.

The Sonics' breakthrough happened in 1974–75. Russell

Lee Winfield, *left*, leaps high for a basket over Fred Carter of the Philadelphia 76ers in 1972.

HINTS OF GREATNESS 17

coached the team to a 43–39 record and its first playoff spot. The team finished strong in the regular season, winning its last seven games. Haywood and Brown each averaged more than 20 points per game. Point guard Slick Watts, known for his distinctive shaved head and headband, ranked in the NBA's top 10 in assists (6.1) and steals (2.3) per game.

The Sonics beat the Detroit Pistons in the first round of the 1975 playoffs. However, they lost a six-game series to the Golden State Warriors in the second round.

Before the 1975–76 season, the Sonics traded their biggest star, Haywood, to the New York Knicks. But Seattle still managed to repeat its record from the season before and returned to the playoffs.

Brown was the top scorer at 23.9 points per game. Four other players averaged in double figures, topped by second-year center Tom Burleson at 15.6 points per game. Burleson, at 7 feet 2 inches, also grabbed 9 rebounds per game and blocked nearly two shots each game. Watts led the NBA in assists (8.1) and steals (3.2) per game. The Sonics did not last long in the 1976 playoffs, though. The Phoenix Suns bounced them in their first-round series.

> ### Which Direction?
>
> Slick Watts was from Mississippi. Before he joined the SuperSonics, Watts was barely even aware of the state of Washington. In fact, when he was headed to Seattle for a tryout, he was surprised to be headed west. "Looking back, I had no relation concerning the Northwest," he said. "I often thought of Washington as Washington DC. When I got the opportunity to come up here, I was surprised that the direction was even going to the West Coast, figuring I was going out East."

The Sonics' Slick Watts (13) leaps to save the ball from going out of bounds during a game against the New York Nets on December 29, 1976.

In 1976–77, the Sonics' modest streak of making the playoffs ended after only two years. At 40–42, they missed the 1977 postseason. Russell resigned as coach and general manager.

The next season did not start out well. Under new coach Bob Hopkins, the Sonics began 5–17. They fired Hopkins and brought back Lenny Wilkens, their former player/coach. This time, however, he was just the coach. Wilkens turned the team around. The SuperSonics qualified for the 1978 playoffs by going 42–18 after Wilkens took over.

The Sonics did not have a player who averaged 20 points per game, but seven men averaged in double figures. Gus Williams led the SuperSonics in scoring at 18.1 points per game. He also averaged 2.3

Dennis Johnson, *left*, makes his pass around the Bullets' Bob Dandridge during Game 6 of the NBA Finals in 1978.

steals per game. Williams combined with Dennis Johnson to give the Sonics a terrific pair of defensive guards.

Brown was still hitting his outside shots and scoring 16.6 points per game. Another addition was Marvin Webster, a 7-foot-1-inch center acquired from the Denver Nuggets. Webster's shot-blocking ability had earned him a nickname "The Human Eraser." Webster grabbed 12.6 rebounds per game. A pair of young and old forwards also bolstered the Sonics' rebounding effort. Rookie Jack Sikma and 14-year veteran Paul Silas each averaged approximately eight rebounds per game.

Under Wilkens, the Sonics continued to thrive in the playoffs. They knocked off the Los Angeles Lakers, the Portland Trail Blazers, and the Denver

> ### Scary Nickname
>
> Marvin Webster, who played one season for the Sonics in 1977–78, had earned the nickname "The Human Eraser" when he was in college. A 7-foot-1 center for Morgan State, Webster intimidated players who came near the basket when he was standing beneath it. Perhaps they were already worried about Webster before he even did anything. Joe O'Brien, the coach of Assumption College, said: "I think our players were intimidated by Webster's nickname as much as anything."

Nuggets. That brought them all the way to the NBA Finals. There, they met the Washington Bullets. The Bullets had the formidable frontcourt of Elvin Hayes, Wes Unseld, and Bob Dandridge. The series went the full seven games.

In Game 4, the Sonics were trying to take a 3–1 series lead. They were playing in Seattle's Kingdome. That was normally the home of Seattle's professional football team, the Seahawks, and its professional baseball team, the Mariners. The SuperSonics' normal arena, the Seattle Coliseum, was unavailable because a mobile home show was booked there.

Seattle fans set an NBA Finals record with an attendance of 39,457. But the visiting Bullets won the game in overtime to tie the series at 2–2. The Sonics came back to win a close Game 5. In Game 6, though, the Bullets won easily to set up a winner-take-all Game 7 in Seattle.

The Sonics cut the Bullets' 11-point lead to four points with 90 seconds left in the game. But the Bullets surged even further ahead. Again, Seattle got the lead down to two. Then, Unseld made two clutch free throws, and the Bullets won the 1978 NBA championship. But the Sonics would be back soon.

CHAPTER 4

CHAMPIONS AT LAST

The 1977–78 season had been a time of success and disappointment for the SuperSonics. They made a surprising run to the NBA Finals, but they lost the championship to the Washington Bullets in a seven-game series.

The disappointment did not show in the Sonics' performance during the 1978–79 regular season, though. They posted their best record yet, 52–30, and finished first in the Pacific Division. Because of the excitement generated by the previous

Playing Smarter

"*The difference from last year is maturity. Last year we were so young, we played on emotion. There were questions. Now we run strictly on confidence.*"
— Coach Lenny Wilkens on his 1978–79 team

Jack Sikma, *left*, blocks a shot by Elvin Hayes of the Washington Bullets as Lonnie Shelton (8) comes in for the rebound.

season's run to the Finals, the Sonics moved all of their home games to the Kingdome. They drew the biggest home crowds in the league, averaging 18,225 fans per game.

The SuperSonics featured basically the same lineup as the previous season. Though they lost center Marvin Webster, they added forward/center Lonnie Shelton. The team featured another balanced scoring lineup. Seven players averaged double figures. Tom LaGarde and John Johnson had 11 points per game. Gus Williams had 19.2 points per game. Jack Sikma grabbed 12.4 rebounds per game. And Paul Silas still averaged 7 rebounds per game, even while playing fewer minutes at age 35.

Silas was important to the team beyond whatever numbers he put in the box score. He was a leader. "Look anywhere on our team, and you'll see Paul's influence," coach Lenny Wilkens said.

The Sonics were the toughest team to score against in the NBA. Their average of 103.9 points allowed per game was the league's lowest. Dennis Johnson led the defense and was named to the NBA's All-Defensive first team.

Seattle's long-range shooting specialist, "Downtown" Freddie Brown, looked ahead to the playoffs and saw a familiar matchup. "Don't be fooling yourself," he said. "You know it all boils down to us against Washington one more time.

> **Not Getting His Due**
>
> A *Sports Illustrated* article once called Sonics guard Gus Williams "perhaps the league's most underrated player, going to the All-Star Game only twice despite scoring more than 18 points per game for seven straight seasons."

Gus Williams holds on to the ball after landing on the floor, while Tom Henderson of the Bullets reaches for it on June 1, 1979.

Both teams have great people all the way through the lineup. They're deeper, but we make up for that with our backcourt."

The Bullets had put together an even better season than the Sonics, going 54–28. And they still had the lineup that had beaten Seattle in the Finals the year before, led by Elvin Hayes and Wes Unseld.

The Sonics eliminated the Los Angeles Lakers in their first playoff series in five games. Then they needed to go the full seven games to get past the Phoenix Suns. That put the SuperSonics back into the NBA Finals against the Bullets.

After Game 1, the Sonics might have wondered about their luck against Washington.

CHAMPIONS AT LAST **25**

Seattle came back from 18 points down to tie the game as time was running out. Dennis Johnson blocked the Bullets' last shot attempt, but he was called for a foul. The Bullets' Larry Wright made two free throws with no time on the clock to give Washington a two-point victory.

However, that was the only game the Bullets would win in the 1979 Finals. The Sonics won the next two games by 10 points each. Game 4 went to overtime. The Sonics had a two-point lead when the Bullets tried one last shot with three seconds left. Dennis Johnson blocked it again, but this time there was no foul.

The Sonics were now ahead in the series three games to one. They needed to win just one more to claim the championship. Seattle clinched the title in Game 5, thanks to a 12–0 scoring run in the third quarter. Brown contributed four key baskets near the end of the game. The Sonics won 97–93 for the NBA title. It was Seattle's first major professional sports championship. Through the 2010–11 NBA season, it remained the city's only one.

A Modest MVP

Dennis Johnson was named MVP of the 1979 NBA Finals. He called himself a "funny-looking black kid with red hair and freckles." The rest of the team was just as funny looking, he said. But more importantly, according to Johnson, the other Sonics worked just as hard as he did.

Seattle coach Lenny Wilkens holds up the NBA championship trophy before fans lining the Seattle streets in celebration of the Sonics' 1979 victory.

CHAMPIONS AT LAST

CHAPTER 5

REGULAR CONTENDERS

By the start of the 1979–80 season, the SuperSonics were firmly established as one of the NBA's premier teams. They had gone to the NBA Finals two years in a row and won the championship in 1979.

The club was in the midst of a long stretch as a playoff contender. Starting in 1977–78, the Sonics would make the playoffs in 19 of the next 25 seasons. They had only four losing records over that same period.

In 1979–80, the year after they won the championship, the Sonics set another team record for victories by going 56–26. They again led the league in attendance, averaging 21,724 fans per game at the Kingdome. The scoring load was still spread out. Six players averaged in double figures. Gus Williams and Dennis Johnson led the way with 22.1 and 19 points per game respectively. However, the Sonics did not return to the NBA Finals that

Jack Sikma (43) gets a shot off over the Boston Celtics' Dave Cowens during a game in 1980.

year. The Los Angeles Lakers eliminated them in the Western Conference finals.

Freddie Brown had to be happy about the rule change that established the three-point shot in 1979–80. In the past, every shot counted as two points, except for free throws. "Downtown" Brown became the NBA's first three-point shooting percentage leader. He made 44.3 percent of his tries that season.

The next season, the SuperSonics toppled from their place among the NBA's better teams. They no longer had their elite backcourt. Johnson was traded to the Phoenix Suns for Paul Westphal, who was injured and missed half of the season. And Williams and the club could not agree on a contract, so he sat out the whole season. The Sonics fell to a 34–48 record and missed the playoffs.

> **Worth Waiting For?**
>
> When the Sonics and star Gus Williams could not agree on a contract, he sat out the entire 1980–81 season. But the holdout proved to be worth it for Williams, who was set up for the rest of his life as a result. As part of the contract he eventually signed, the Sonics placed money into a fund and guaranteed that Williams would receive $250,000 a year for the rest of his life starting at age 38.

However, the SuperSonics rebounded to a 52–30 record in 1981–82. Williams returned to score 23.4 points per game. Jack Sikma averaged nearly 20 points and 13 rebounds per game. Williams ranked seventh in the league in scoring, and Sikma was second in rebounding. The Sonics made it to the second round of the playoffs before losing to the San Antonio Spurs.

For the next two years, the Sonics played well in the

Lonnie Shelton (8) finds himself surrounded by Milwaukee Bucks after grabbing a key rebound in the final minutes of a playoff game in 1980.

regular season, but they could not seem to get out of the first round of the playoffs. Brown retired at the end of 1983–84. After 13 seasons, he left as the team's all-time leader in games and points. The team did not even make it to the playoffs during the next two seasons. Bernie Bickerstaff replaced Lenny Wilkens as coach for 1985–86.

Under Bickerstaff, the 1986–87 team improved to only 39–43, but that was good enough to make the playoffs. Once in the postseason, the Sonics made it to the Western Conference finals before losing to the Lakers.

The SuperSonics featured three high-scoring forwards. Dale Ellis, who came in a trade with the Dallas Mavericks,

Dale Ellis (3) finds his path to the basket blocked by Reggie Miller, *left*, of the Indiana Pacers on February 28, 1989.

built his average of 24.9 points per game on three-point shooting. Tom Chambers scored 23.3 points per game. Xavier McDaniel averaged 23 points per game. The Sonics became the first team in NBA history with three players to average at least 23 points a game in a season.

In the next two seasons, the Sonics returned to winning records at 44–38 and 47–35 respectively. Ellis was third in the league in scoring in 1988–89. Seattle made the playoffs both seasons, but got no further than the second round either time.

Seattle's playoff run ended in 1989–90 with a 41–41 record. That was also Bickerstaff's last season as the Sonics' coach. He was replaced by K. C. Jones. Jones directed the team to the same record the next season.

That got the Sonics back into the playoffs. But they lasted only one round.

Coach Jones lasted just 36 games into 1991–92. After four games with an interim head coach, George Karl was installed as the new coach. He led the team to a 27–15 finish for a 47–35 overall record. Though neither Eddie Johnson nor Shawn Kemp started most of the time, they provided offense off the bench and combined to average more than 32 points per game. Kemp, an athletic, 6-foot-10 forward/center, blocked nearly two shots and averaged more than 10 rebounds per game. That year, the Sonics reached the second round of the playoffs. It was also Gary Payton's second season in the league. The Sonics had picked him second overall in the 1990 NBA Draft, but the young player had not

FROM SPAIN TO THE NBA

Before the Sonics hired George Karl as coach in 1992, he was coaching a Spanish basketball team called Real Madrid. Previously, Karl had been an NBA coach with two teams, but no other NBA jobs were coming his way.

"I thought my NBA door was closed," Karl said. However, the Sonics decided to give him another chance, hiring him to take over after firing K. C. Jones. He had to readjust to being back in the United States. "I was just back from Spain, and I was speaking Spanish on the sidelines," Karl said. "And I was thinking to myself, 'Wow, these guys are really going to think I'm smart.'" Karl went on to have a 384–150 record over his six and a half seasons with the Sonics. After Lenny Wilkens, that was the longest any coach stayed with the team.

> ### That Tight Defense
>
> Gary Payton was so known for his tough defense that he got the nickname "The Glove." The story is that after seeing Payton shut down the Phoenix Suns' Kevin Johnson, Payton's cousin told him he was "holding Johnson like a baseball in a glove."

performed up to everyone's high expectations. He would mature, though.

Karl's first full season as coach was 1992–93. The Sonics went 55–27 and earned a spot in the postseason. The Sonics made it past the Utah Jazz and the Houston Rockets in the first two rounds of the playoffs. Then the Phoenix Suns beat them in a seven-game Western Conference finals.

The SuperSonics ran through the league to begin 1993–94. In a trade with the Indiana Pacers, the club added Detlef Schrempf. He had previously won the NBA's Sixth Man Award for his play off the bench. The Sonics won 20 of their first 22 games and finished with a league-best 63–19 record. That was the team's highest-ever win total. Like previous Sonics teams, the scoring was spread around to six players who averaged double figures. The team also led the league in steals.

When it came to the postseason, the Sonics suffered a first-round upset and were ousted by the Denver Nuggets. The same thing happened the next season. They had a fine regular-season record, but they lost again in the first round of the playoffs.

The 1995–96 season would be different, though. The Sonics were consistent throughout the regular season and suffered only one two-game losing streak. They achieved

Detlef Schrempf celebrates the Sonics' lead with less than three seconds left on the clock against the Utah Jazz on May 20, 1996 in Seattle.

their best record in team history at 64–18. Still, that was overshadowed by the Chicago Bulls' 72–10 record. Kemp scored 19.6 points per game and Payton netted 19.3 points per game. Those stats earned the duo the nickname the "Sonic Boom" for their powerful scoring abilities. Payton also grabbed nearly three steals and handed out 7.5 assists per game. Guard Hersey Hawkins added 15.6 points per game.

The Sonics came through in the 1996 postseason. They reached the NBA Finals, where they faced off against the powerful, Michael Jordan-led Bulls. They took Chicago to six games before losing the series, but they had finally silenced the talk about how they could not win in the postseason.

CHAPTER 6

NEW CITY, NEW FUTURE

After losing to the Chicago Bulls in the 1996 NBA Finals, the Sonics continued to maintain their high standard of play. In the next two seasons, they won 57 and 61 games respectively. That gave them an eight-season streak of making the postseason.

They did not return to the Finals in 1997 or 1998, though. They lost each season in the second round of the playoffs.

Shawn Kemp left Seattle after the 1996–97 season. He was part of a three-team trade that ended up giving the SuperSonics Vin Baker. He was another forward who could put up good scoring numbers. In Baker's first season in Seattle, 1997–98, he and Gary Payton each averaged 19.2 points per game. Baker made three game-winning shots with the clock running out that season.

The Sonics' playoff streak ended in the 1998–99 season. They made it back to the playoffs in 1999–2000 with a 45–37 record. Payton had the

Gary Payton (20) goes for a layup against the Houston Rockets' Juaquin Hawkins in the fourth quarter of the Sonics' 104-97 win on November 5, 2002.

Sonics forward Vin Baker (42) attempts to block a shot by Shaquille O'Neal of the Los Angeles Lakers during a 1998 playoff game.

highest-scoring season of his career with 24.2 points per game, while still averaging 8.9 assists per game. But the Utah Jazz knocked the Sonics from the playoffs in the first round.

Having nearly the same record the next season was not enough to get the Sonics into the playoffs, but they did return a year later, in 2001–02. The Sonics went 45–37 in the first full season under new coach Nate McMillan. He was a former Seattle player who had replaced Paul Westphal early in 2000–01. In his fourth NBA season, Rashard Lewis became the Sonics' number-two scorer at 16.8 points per game. Lewis was a 6-foot-10 forward who got most of his points from outside shooting. But again, the playoffs were

> ### Unhappy Kemp
>
> The SuperSonics had to trade away Shawn Kemp after the 1996–97 season because he had become unhappy with the team. Kemp was upset when the Sonics signed free agent Jim McIlvaine to a far bigger contract than his own. After playing one more season in Seattle, Kemp said he would not return for another. He would not take any phone calls from the team—not even from his teammates. The Sonics ultimately traded Kemp to the Cleveland Cavaliers.

another one-round-and-out trip for Seattle.

After 2001–02, the Sonics made the playoffs only once in their last six years in Seattle. That came in 2004–05, with a 52–30 regular-season record. It was good enough to win the new Northwest Division. However, the Sonics' look had changed.

Their constant force in the backcourt, Payton, had been traded in 2003 to the Milwaukee Bucks. In exchange, the Sonics got Ray Allen. He was one of the NBA's best outside shooters. Allen and Lewis pumped in jump shots, with Allen netting 23.9 points and Lewis averaging 20.5 points per game. The Sonics beat the Sacramento Kings in the opening round of the 2005 playoffs, but they fell to the San Antonio Spurs in the second. After the season, the SuperSonics lost their coach. McMillan's contract had run out, and he instead signed with the Portland Trail Blazers.

By 2005–06, rumors were flying about the team's possible departure from Seattle. In the Sonics' last three seasons there, they won just 35, 31, and 20 games respectively. Allen and Lewis kept playing well. Allen averaged 25.1 points per game in 2005–06 and 26.4 in 2006–07. But he was traded to the Boston Celtics in June 2007. Lewis had seasons averaging

20.1 and 22.4 points per game. But Lewis was traded to the Orlando Magic in the summer of 2007.

The team's final season in Seattle marked the NBA arrival of Kevin Durant. Durant averaged 20.3 points per game his first year and was named the Rookie of the Year. That at least gave Seattle fans a reason to cheer during a depressing season.

After struggling through their first season in Oklahoma City, the Thunder were more than respectable in 2009–10. They went 50–32 and made the playoffs. Durant led the league in scoring at 30.1 points per game. The Thunder's point guard, Russell Westbrook, drew raves around the league for his play in his second season. He often showed up on television highlights with strong drives to the basket. Westbrook averaged 16.1 points and eight assists per game.

In the 2010 playoffs, the Thunder faced the defending champion Los Angeles Lakers. Many were excited to see the battle between the Thunder's up-and-coming Durant and the Lakers' superstar Kobe Bryant. The Thunder gave the Lakers a scare but were ultimately eliminated in six games.

Oklahoma City came back strong in 2010–11. Led by Durant and Westbrook, the Thunder tallied 55 wins in the regular season. That was the team's most since moving to

> **Home-Court Advantage**
>
> "*It's sort of like an ant hill where the ants are coming in. The fans of Oklahoma City are sort of pouring into this palace.*"
> —NBA commissioner David Stern on the atmosphere at the Thunder's first playoff game

Thunder forward Kevin Durant keeps the ball away from Los Angeles Lakers guard Kobe Bryant during a first-round playoff series in 2010.

Oklahoma City. The record was also good enough to earn the team its first Northwest Division title and another berth in the playoffs.

In the first round, the Thunder easily beat the Denver Nuggets squad 4–1. They faced the Memphis Grizzlies in the second round. The Thunder came out on top with 105–90 win over Memphis in Game 7. In the Western Conference finals, the veteran-filled Dallas Mavericks defeated the Thunder four games to one.

Although the Thunder had fallen just short, it was hard for fans to be too disappointed. Many felt the team was still a few seasons away from being among the NBA's elite. But behind Durant, Westbrook, and others, the Thunder showed that the team of the future was already in a position to shine.

TIMELINE

1966	Seattle is awarded an NBA franchise.
1967	The Seattle SuperSonics play their first game on October 13.
1968	The Sonics trade Walt Hazzard to the Atlanta Hawks for Lenny Wilkens.
1970	The Sonics sign Spencer Haywood.
1972	Sonics coach and guard Lenny Wilkens is traded to the Cleveland Cavaliers after Sonics owner Sam Schulman insists he choose between coaching and playing.
1973	Spencer Haywood scores 51 points against the Kansas City-Omaha Kings on January 3.
1974	Guard Fred Brown scores 58 points against the Golden State Warriors on March 23.
1975	The Sonics trade Spencer Haywood to the New York Knicks.
1979	The Sonics defeat the Washington Bullets to clinch their first and only NBA championship.
1987	Nate McMillan ties the NBA rookie record with 25 assists in a game against the Los Angeles Clippers on February 23.

1988	Dale Ellis scores 47 points against the San Antonio Spurs on January 9, one game after Tom Chambers had scored 46 points against the Houston Rockets.
1989	The Sonics lose a five-overtime game to the Milwaukee Bucks 155–154. Dale Ellis scores 53 points.
1999	The Sonics go 25–25 in a season shortened to 50 games due to labor problems between the NBA and its players. Seattle misses the playoffs for the first time in eight years.
2006	The SuperSonics announce the sale of the team to a group from Oklahoma City.
2008	The NBA grants permission for the club's owners to move the SuperSonics to Oklahoma City.
2008	The Thunder play their first official NBA game in Oklahoma City on October 29. They lose to the Milwaukee Bucks, 98–87.
2010	The team makes its first playoff appearance in five years but loses in the first round.
2011	The Thunder go 55–27 during the regular season, their best record since the team had won 61 games as the SuperSonics in 1997–98.
2011	The Thunder reach the Western Conference finals before falling to the Dallas Mavericks in five games.

QUICK STATS

FRANCHISE HISTORY
Seattle SuperSonics (1967–2008)
Oklahoma City Thunder (2008–)

NBA FINALS
(win in bold)
1978, **1979**, 1996

CONFERENCE TITLES
1978, 1979, 1996

DIVISION TITLES
1979, 1994, 1996, 1997, 1998, 2005, 2011

KEY PLAYERS
(postion[s]; years with the team)
Ray Allen (G; 2002–07)
Freddie Brown (G; 1971–84)
Tom Chambers (F; 1983–88)
Kevin Durant (F; 2007–)
Spencer Haywood (F; 1971–75)
Dennis Johnson (G; 1976–80)
Shawn Kemp (F/C; 1989–97)
Rashard Lewis (F; 1999–2007)
Xavier McDaniel (F; 1985–91)
Nate McMillan (G; 1986–98)
Gary Payton (G; 1990–2003)
Bob Rule (C/F; 1967–71)
Jack Sikma (C/F; 1977–86)
Slick Watts (G; 1973–78)
Russell Westbrook (G; 2008–)
Gus Williams (G; 1977–84)

KEY COACHES
George Karl (1992–98):
   384–150, 40–40 (postseason)
Nate McMillan (2000–05):
   212–183, 8–8 (postseason)
Lenny Wilkens (1969–72, 1977–85):
   478–402, 37–32 (postseason)

HOME ARENAS
Seattle Coliseum (1967–78, 1985–94)
Kingdome (1978–85)
Tacoma Dome (1994–95)
KeyArena (1995–2008)
Ford Center (2008–)

*All statistics through 2010–11 season

QUOTES AND ANECDOTES

Lenny Wilkens was unhappy about how he was treated by the SuperSonics when they decided to trade him to the Cleveland Cavaliers. "I had heard rumors I was going to be traded," he said. "I asked our front office about it. They denied it, so I took them at their word. And then, my father-in-law called me and told me I had been traded to Cleveland the day before they told me."

"I was a little shocked, I guess, by his stubbornness. I still think it was wrong. But it's history. It was a very unfortunate experience, but I hold no vindictiveness. He had his position, and I had mine." — Sonics owner Sam Schulman on Gus Williams' holdout, which lasted a whole season

At the 2001 All-Star Weekend, Desmond Mason, a 6-foot-7 forward, became the first Sonics player to win the dunk contest.

"It's a good basketball city. And I think the roots and the soul of the game of basketball should be respected a little bit more." — Former Sonics coach George Karl on Seattle, explaining what a professional basketball team meant to Seattle

The Thunder trailed the Denver Nuggets by nine points with less than four minutes left in Game 5 of their 2011 first-round playoff series. "I just told myself . . . I got to get us going," said forward Kevin Durant. "Russell (Westbrook) and myself are the leaders of this team and he looked at me and said, 'This is what you do.' And I just said all right. And I just kept going." Durant scored the team's final nine points of the game to help the Thunder win 100–97 and clinch the series. In all, Durant scored 41 points in the game.

GLOSSARY

assist

A pass that leads directly to a made basket.

backcourt

The point guards and shooting guards on a basketball team.

contract

A binding agreement about, for example, years of commitment by a basketball player in exchange for a given salary.

draft

A system used by professional sports leagues to select new players in order to spread incoming talent among all teams. The NBA Draft is held each June.

expansion

In sports, the addition of a franchise or franchises to a league.

franchise

An entire sports organization, including the players, coaches, and staff.

free agent

A player whose contract has expired and who is able to sign with a team of his choice.

general manager

The executive who is in charge of the team's overall operation. He or she hires and fires coaches, drafts players, and signs free agents.

postseason

The games in which the best teams play after the regular-season schedule has been completed.

rebound

To secure the basketball after a missed shot.

resign

To give up a job or position.

rookie

A first-year player in the NBA.

roster

The players as a whole on a basketball team.

FOR MORE INFORMATION

Further Reading

Ballard, Chris. *The Art of a Beautiful Game: The Thinking Fan's Tour of the NBA.* New York: Simon & Schuster, 2009.

Hubbard, Jan (editor). *The Official NBA Encyclopedia.* New York: Doubleday, 2000.

Simmons, Bill. *The Book of Basketball: The NBA According to the Sports Guy.* New York: Random House, 2009.

Web Links

To learn more about the Oklahoma City Thunder, visit ABDO Publishing Company online at **www.abdopublishing.com**. Web sites about the Thunder are featured on our Book Links page. These links are routinely monitored and updated to provide the most current information available.

Places To Visit

KeyArena
305 Harrison Street
Seattle, WA 98109
405-602-8700
www.keyarena.com
This was the Seattle SuperSonics' home from 1995 until the team left for Oklahoma City in 2008.

Naismith Memorial Basketball Hall of Fame
1000 West Columbus Avenue
Springfield, MA 01105
413-781-6500
www.hoophall.com
This hall of fame and museum highlights the greatest players and moments in the history of basketball. Former Sonics player and coach Lenny Wilkens is enshrined here.

Oklahoma City Arena
100 West Reno Avenue
Oklahoma City, OK 73102
www.theokcarena.com
405-602-8700
This has been the Thunder's home arena since 2008. The team plays 41 regular-season games here each year. Tours are available when the Thunder are not playing.

INDEX

Allen, Ray, 39

Baker, Vin, 37
Barry, Brent, 9
Bennett, Clay (owner), 6
Bickerstaff, Bernie (coach), 31–32
Brooks, Scott (coach), 9
Brown, Freddie, 17–18, 20, 24, 26, 30–31
Buckwalter, Bucky (coach), 17
Burleson, Tom, 18

Carlesimo, P. J. (coach), 9
Chambers, Tom, 32

Durant, Kevin, 6, 9, 40–41

Ellis, Dale, 31–32

Ford Center, 8

Green, Jeff, 9

Hawkins, Hersey, 35
Haywood, Spencer, 13–15, 17–18
Hazzard, Walt, 11–12
Hopkins, Bob (coach), 19

Johnson, Dennis, 20, 24, 26, 29–30
Johnson, Eddie, 33
Johnson, John, 24
Jones, K. C., 32–33

Karl, George (coach), 33–34
Kemp, Shawn, 33, 35, 37, 39
KeyArena, 7
Kingdome, 21, 24, 29

LaGarde, Tom, 24
Lewis, Rashard, 38–40

McDaniel, Xavier, 32
McIlvaine, Jim, 39
McMillan, Nate (coach), 38–39

NBA Finals
    1978, 21
    1979, 25–26
    1996, 35, 37
Nissalke, Tom (coach), 17

Payton, Gary, 33, 34, 35, 37, 39

Rule, Bob, 11–13
Russell, Bill (coach and general manager), 17, 19

Schrempf, Detlef, 34
Schulman, Sam (owner), 14–15
Seattle Coliseum, 21
Shelton, Lonnie, 24
Shultz, Howard (owner), 6
Sikma, Jack, 20, 24, 30
Silas, Paul, 20, 24
Snyder, Dick, 13

Watts, Slick, 18
Webster, Marvin, 20, 21, 24
Westbrook, Russell, 9, 40–41
Westphal, Paul, 30, 38
Wilkens, Lenny (player and coach), 12–15, 19–20, 23, 24, 31, 33
Williams, Gus, 19–20, 24, 29–30

About the Author

Ray Frager is a freelance writer based in the Baltimore, Maryland, area. He has been a professional sports editor and writer since 1980. He has worked for the *Trenton Times*, the *Dallas Morning News*, the *Baltimore Sun*, FOXSports.com, and Comcast SportsNet. At the *Sun*, he edited books on Cal Ripken Jr., the building of Baltimore's football stadium, and the Baltimore Ravens' 2000 Super Bowl season. He has also written books on the Baltimore Orioles and the Pittsburgh Pirates.

JAN / 2012